T0113546

RED TAIL DOWN

JOHN J. SCULLY JR.

Archway Publishing books may be ordered through booksellers or by contacting:

Archway Publishing
1663 Liberty Drive
Bloomington, IN 47403
www.archwaypublishing.com
844-669-3957

ISBN: 978-1-6657-4816-2 (sc)
ISBN: 978-1-6657-4817-9 (e)

Library of Congress Control Number: 2023914872

Print information available on the last page.

Archway Publishing rev. date: 09/15/2023

Cast: Heinrich Schmitt
Irene Schmitt
David Taylor
Waldo

April 29 of 1945

[An automobile is traveling on a desolate stretch of road in Southwest Germany. A plane is descending rapidly above the automobile. The motor of the plane is sputtering, and one side of its landing gear is not fully extended to its proper position. The plane crash-lands a short distance ahead of the automobile. The right wing of the plane catches on fire after the hard landing. The driver of the automobile pulls up to the crash site, jumps out of his car, and runs toward the burning plane.]

ACT ONE

SCENE 1 ▬▬▬▬▬▬▬▬▬▬

Heinrich: Are you okay? Can you move?

David: I can move. My seat belt buckle is jammed. I'm going to have to cut the seat belt with my knife to get out of here.

Heinrich: Let me do it; I'll have a better angle at it.

David: Here, take my knife, go ahead.

[David hands Heinrich his knife. Heinrich cuts through the seat belt to free up David.]

Heinrich: That should do it. You should be able to get out now.

David: Thanks.

[The pilot steps out of the cockpit onto the wing of the plane, then jumps to the ground. He's limping and his head is bleeding as he steps away from the plane.]

Heinrich: We need to get out of here quickly. We'll be in great danger if we don't leave now.

David: I've got a rucksack in the cockpit; let me get it.

Heinrich: You're limping, let me get it for you. We have no time to waste. Please go to the car now, get in the back seat, and stay low.

[The pilot hobbles to the car and climbs into the back seat. The driver of the car returns quickly with the rucksack and jumps into the front seat, puts the car in gear, and drives away immediately. There's a dog in the back seat.]

David: Who's this guy?

Heinrich: That's Waldo. Don't worry, he doesn't bite. Please stay down low.

[They're only a short distance away when the burning plane explodes. The pilot lifts himself up to look out the back window at the charred wreckage.]

David: You just saved my life.

Heinrich: Stay down. Do not lift your head up again for any reason.

David: Sorry, it won't happen again.

[They continue driving until they reach a secluded area. They turn into a driveway and arrive at a house surrounded by woods. The driver turns off the car.]

Heinrich: You can get up now.

David: Where are we?

Heinrich: It's our summer home. It's where I come with my family to get away from it all. The nearest house is a 15-minute walk from here. You should be safe here.

David: Is anyone inside?

Heinrich: Just my wife. You have nothing to worry about. The kitchen is in the back of the house…she's probably cooking and didn't hear us come up the driveway. Let's walk to the porch and I'll stick my head inside the door to let her know I have someone with me.

[They walk to the porch together. Heinrich sticks his head in the door to announce his arrival. David stands behind him and off to the side unseen by his wife.]

Heinrich: Irene, ich bin zu hause und habe jemanden mitgebracht.

[Irene, I'm home! And I've brought a guest with me.]

Irene: Ein Gast, ohne mir vorher bescheid zu sagen von wo?

(A guest with no warning…from where?)

Heinrich: Er ist einfach irgendwie bei mir vorbeigekommen.

(He kind of just dropped in on me.)

[Both men then step into the house together. When Irene first sees the bleeding pilot she appears shocked, but quickly recovers.]

Irene: This man's head is bleeding. We have a first aid kit in the car. Why have you not bandaged his head?

Heinrich: His plane crashed near me while I was driving here. I didn't have much time to look him over before we had to get out of there. I was trying to save his life.

Irene: And having him bleed to death while you drove him here would've been saving his life?

Heinrich: There wasn't much time, honey. The Gestapo or the SS could've arrived at any moment.

Irene: All right Heinrich, please get me a bowl of water and some towels from the kitchen. I'll need to get some bandages and antiseptic from the medicine cabinet. What is our guest's name?

Heinrich: I never got around to asking him his name.

Irene: You don't know our guest's name?

Heinrich: We didn't have much time to exchange pleasantries when we met.

David: My name's David Taylor, ma'am.

Irene: My name is Irene; this is my husband, Heinrich.

David: Nice to meet you.

Irene: Please have a seat here while we get what we need to patch you up.

[Irene and Heinrich leave the room and return quickly with their supplies.]

Irene: Close your eyes, I'll need to wash the cut and take a closer look at it. [Irene washes and inspects the cut.] You could use a few stitches, but we'll have to make do with bandages. I'm going to apply some antiseptic—this might sting a little.

David: Go ahead.

[Irene applies the ointment to the cut.]

Irene: All right, that should do it. I'll need to wrap a bandage around your head now.

David: I'm ready.

Irene: That should do it. You were limping when you came in the door. You've injured your leg, too?

David: Yes I must've smashed my left knee into the control panels when I crash-landed.

Irene: Can you roll up your pant leg, I want to take a look at it.

David: Sure.

Irene: It's very swollen. Your knee looks to be about twice the size of what it normally should be. Does anything feel broken?

David: I don't think anything's broken. I think I just banged it up badly.

Irene: You'll need to keep that leg elevated. We'll have you stay in the guest room. Heinrich, please take him to the bed in the guest room while I get some extra pillows to elevate his leg.

Heinrich: Follow me, David.

[Heinrich leads David into the guest room.]

David: Let me sit in that chair first. I'd like to at least take my boots off if you're going to put me in that bed.

Heinrich: Good idea.

[After sitting down, David removes his right boot relatively easily, but writhes in pain while trying to remove the one on his injured left leg.]

Heinrich: Let me help you with that?

David: I can get it.

[Irene returns with a handful of pillows.]

Irene: Come lie down in the bed and I'll prop your leg up with these pillows.

Heinrich: I think he's in more pain than he's letting on.

Irene: I can see that. Applying some ice to his knee would do him some good, but where would we get ice in late April?

David: Don't worry, I'll be okay.

Irene: Elevating it should help a great deal. Are you hungry? I have food on the stove.

David: I haven't eaten since I left my base early this morning.

Irene: You must be hungry then. The food is warm, it'll only take me a minute to prepare a plate for you. Would you like some red wine with your meal? It's either that or water.

David: Water would be fine, ma'am.

[Irene exits the room.]

David: You're a lucky guy to have a wife like that.

Heinrich: Yes she's my better half by a long shot.

[Irene returns with a tray of food and a glass of water.]

Irene: No need to move. This tray is made for eating in bed. I can rest it right where you are.

David: Thank you. This looks delicious.

Irene: Where would you like to eat your meal, Heinrich?

Heinrich: I'd like to eat in here with David if he doesn't mind.

Irene: Perhaps David would like to eat his meal alone. He's been through much today.

David: No, not at all. I'd much prefer for all of us to eat together. I can hobble out to your dining room table, and we can all eat there.

Irene: Don't you dare move. Heinrich, how does your arm feel today?

Heinrich: I still have numbness in my hand, it's better than it was though.

Irene: Can you bring the chair and ottoman in from the other room?

Heinrich: Yes I can do that.

Irene: Good; and there are some small linens on the bottom shelf of the linen closet. Could you get one—we'll cover the ottoman with it and use it as our table, so we can all eat here together. You can start without us, David.

David: I'd much rather wait for both of you to join me.

Irene: All right we'll be back in just a minute. Heinrich, after you've brought the chair and ottoman in, could you please fill a pitcher of water and bring two more glasses with it.

Heinrich: Got it, honey.

[Irene and Heinrich return with everything they need, and they all start eating together.]

David: This food is delicious ma'am.

Irene: Thank you. I'm going to close this door. I left Waldo a big bowl of food—he'll devour it and then come in here looking for more. Our Waldo has an insatiable appetite.

David: He sounds like my dog back home.

Irene: He likes to jump up on that bed, too. I'm sure he'll knock your tray over if he does it.

David: I'm not taking Waldo's bed away from him am I?

Irene: Don't worry about it. How does your knee feel?

David: Elevating it has taken some of the throbbing away. I'll be okay.

Irene: You've nearly finished everything on your plate. Let me get you some more.

David: No thank you, ma'am, you put a lot on the plate. I'm full.

Irene: Suit yourself, but you must have a piece of strudel for dessert.

Heinrich: Yes you must have some strudel. My wife makes the best strudel in all of Germany.

David: Well, if you insist, I can always make some room for dessert.

Irene: Yes, we insist. The strudel is warm and ready to serve. Would you like coffee or tea with it?

David: Whatever you're having, I'll have.

Irene: Tea it is. Heinrich, help me carry these dirty dishes to the kitchen and we'll be right back with dessert and tea.

[The two return shortly with the strudel and three cups of tea.]

David: I'm curious, how is it that both of you speak such flawless English?

Heinrich: My wife speaks several languages fluently. She taught French and English at the university prior to the war. Unfortunately, the university where she taught closed after the war started.

Irene: And my Heinrich spent time in your country as an exchange student at Harvard.

David: A Harvard guy, huh. Small world. I grew up in South Boston.

Heinrich: I was only at Harvard for a year as an exchange student.

David: Did you like it there?

Heinrich: Yes, it was a very nice experience.

David: This strudel is very good.

Heinrich: I told you it's the best in Germany.

Irene: All we need now is our Hans and Helga to be here to share this strudel with us.

Heinrich: Don't worry honey, they'll be home soon. This awful war is almost over. [Heinrich puts his arm around his wife to console her.]

Irene: From your mouth to God's ears, Heinrich. Our two children are staying with an aunt in Switzerland.

We should've brought them here instead of sending them to Switzerland.

Heinrich: You know that wasn't possible at the time, Irene.

Irene: There were constant air raids in Munich where we live. Sirens would go off in the middle of the night, we'd have to run to air raid shelters.

There was no sleep. The bombs kept landing closer and closer to our home and we were never sure if the next bomb would land right on our home. My husband was away at war, so we had to go through it all without him.

David: I'm sorry you had to go through all that.

Irene: It's not your fault. I have a civil service job in the city that's considered essential. I'm obligated to be there every day. Commuting from here in the mountains to my job in the city every day would've been nearly impossible. And that's when we decided to send our children to Switzerland. It was a very difficult decision for us.

Heinrich: We had to pull some strings at the foreign office to get our children travel visas, including bribing a high-ranking official. We got them there though.

Irene: I want them back so badly.

David: How old are your children?

Irene: Hans is six and Helga is four now.

David: How long have they been in Switzerland?

Heinrich: It's been a little over a year now.

Irene: It's been 371 days and four hours, give or take an hour, since they've left Munich on the train.

Heinrich: My wife has been keeping track on a calendar.

Irene: I'll be right back.

[Irene leaves the room and returns with a photo album.]

Irene: This is our Hans and Helga. The photo was taken right before they left for Switzerland.

David: You've got nice-looking kids.

Irene: Thank you. Waiting for their return is what keeps us going. I can't wait to hug them again and see how much they've grown in a year.

Heinrich: It'll be soon, honey.

Irene: This is a photo of the four of us together.

David: Great-looking family.

Irene: Are you married, David?

David: Yes I got married a few months before I deployed overseas. No children yet though. My wife and I decided to put off starting a family until I returned home.

Irene: Here's a photo of Hans and Helga with my brother Joseph. He looks so happy to be with his niece and nephew, doesn't he. I wish he were here with us, too.

Heinrich: Joseph is a prisoner of war. The Americans captured him in North Africa. It's been a little over two years now since he was captured. He's being held in America.

Irene: He's in South Carolina. I believe the name of the town where he's being held is Walterboro.

David: I take it you've heard from him since he's been captured?

Irene: Yes, he's been allowed to write home and he says he's being treated fairly. We're thankful for that. I want him home though. I want all of us to be back together again.

Heinrich: We'll all be together again soon, honey.

Irene: I suppose I shouldn't complain. There are so many who've lost so much more than we have from this awful war.

David: You said that you were obligated to be at your job every day. Will you have to return there soon?

Irene: I'm not sure. The building I work in was destroyed by bombing a little over a week ago.

Heinrich: The bombing took place at night, so thankfully my wife wasn't in the building at the time.

Irene: It's not the first building I've worked in that's been destroyed by allied bombing. They keep improvising with new places for us to work. They may have already found some underground tunnel for us to work in. I don't know if I'm going back—they may have to come looking for me this time.

David: Again, I'm so sorry to hear you've had to go through all this.

Irene: It's been a long day for you. Perhaps we should let you get some rest.

David: It's up to you. I can't thank the both of you enough for what you've done for me.

Irene: No need to thank us. It's how all people should treat each other. C'mon Heinrich, let's get rid of these dishes and let our guest rest. You must have an extra pair of pajamas you could lend David.

Heinrich: Yes, I think I do.

Irene: Good night, David.

Heinrich: I'll be back in a minute.

[Heinrich and Irene remove the dishes and leave the room. Heinrich returns carrying a folded pair of faded blue pajamas and a cane.]

Heinrich: Here you can put these on if you want. I also found a cane that might help you get around. The bathroom is right outside your bedroom door. We sleep on the second floor, so you'll have the ground floor to yourself after we go upstairs.

David: Thanks, again, for what you've done for me.

Heinrich: No need to thank me. You get some rest now.

SCENE 2 ▰▰▰▰▰▰▰▰▰▰▰▰

[It's the following morning. Heidrich knocks on the door of David's room.]

Heinrich: Are you awake in there?

David: Yes, I'm awake. Come on in.

[Heinrich enters the room. David is out of bed and sitting in a chair.]

Heinrich: You're out of bed I see.

David: Yeah I really don't like staying in bed all day. My knee still hurts, but I can get around some.

Heinrich: I see you're in your flight suit and those pajamas look as if they're in the same place I left them.

David: I appreciate your bringing them in. I stripped down and slept in my skivvies last night. And I'd prefer to have my uniform on now.

Heinrich: I'd probably do the same. Would you like a cup of coffee?

David: Yes, please. I like coffee in the morning.

Heinrich: Good. There's a pot of coffee on the stove, I'll be right back with a cup for you. My wife is making breakfast.

[Heinrich returns with the coffee. Irene follows him with two plates of food.]

Irene: Heinrich has informed me that you're out of bed. I've brought scrambled eggs and bacon for you. I hope you like it.

David: It looks great. I'm sure I will. Thank you.

Irene: Is your leg any better today?

David: I'll be all right, and I can get around okay on it.

Irene: Here's breakfast for the both of you. I want to take Waldo for a walk so why don't you two eat together.

Heinrich: Why don't you wait until I'm finished with my breakfast, and I'll go with you.

Irene: No, Heinrich, you stay here and keep David company. It's been almost a week since I've seen Waldo and I'd like to take him for a walk by myself.

Heinrich: All right, but don't go too far.

Irene: We won't see any people in the direction I'm taking him, and Waldo will chase the wild animals away. You two enjoy your breakfast and you can exchange flying stories while I'm out.

Heinrich: All right, honey, but don't be gone too long or I'll start to worry.

Irene: Don't worry about me. This might be the safest neighborhood in all of Germany right now.

David: Enjoy your walk, ma'am.

Irene: Thank you, David. I will.

[Irene exits.]

David: Did I just hear your wife say that we could exchange flying stories?

Heinrich: Yes you did.

David: So, you're a pilot, too?

Heinrich: Yes I am.

David: You're Luftwaffe?

Heinrich: Right, again.

David: Fighters or bombers?

Heinrich: Fighters, like yourself. I would've told you in the car yesterday, but I thought it might've made you nervous.

David: Are you on leave now—is that why you're out of uniform?

Heinrich: I took a bullet to my forearm about six weeks ago. It happened during a dogfight. The bullet broke a bone in my wrist. I got my cast removed in Munich yesterday, just a few hours before our paths crossed.

David: Your wife mentioned something about your arm last night. You must be healing okay if your cast was taken off after six weeks.

Heinrich: I've lost some feeling in my right hand. It wasn't a direct hit. The bullet glanced off the bone or it would've been a lot worse. If numbness in my right hand is the worst damage I have coming out of this war, I'll consider myself lucky.

David: Will you be expected to report back to your unit soon?

Heinrich: My commanding officer knows my cast was removed yesterday so I've been given another week to recover. If I were to return now the numbness in my right hand might make it difficult for me to control the stick. I'm hoping the war will be over before I have to return.

David: Do you really think the war might be over that soon?

Heinrich: The Russians have Berlin surrounded. Our army is nearly out of ammunition. I have no idea how they're still holding out. So yes, I think this war might be over soon.

David: You got to me very quickly after I landed yesterday, or should I say crash-landed yesterday.

Heinrich: We were both going in the same direction, that was by pure chance. The second I heard your plane overhead, I knew you were in trouble. A plane descending with engine trouble has an unmistakable sound. A sound that I know all too well. Do you know what it was that caused you to force land yesterday?

David: I was in a dogfight about 15 minutes prior to bringing the plane down. It was one of your 109s I was up against, and we both got some close-range shots at each other. One of his shots must've pierced my oil pump or something, I had no oil pressure at all when I brought the plane down.

Heinrich: Did you realize your landing gear wasn't fully extended before you landed?

David: Yes, we have indicator lights in the mustangs that showed something wasn't right with the landing gear. There's a way to get the landing gear down manually but I couldn't get it done on time. By the time I realized it, I was already too low to jump, so I had to land it as best as I could.

Heinrich: It was a nice landing considering what you were up against.

David: What made you stop for me yesterday? You were obviously taking a big risk doing so.

Heinrich: This war is almost over. One more dead pilot is the last thing I'd want to see, if there was anything I could do about it.

David: You did something about it all right.

Heinrich: I've been up against your Red Tails before. I have a story to tell about it, too.

David: Uh-oh.

Heinrich: No worries. We may be enemies in the sky but we're friends here.

David: So what happened?

Heinrich: Last August, my unit was sent up to intercept heavy bombers from your air force that were on their way to bomb the Ploesti oil refineries. The bombers were being escorted by your Red Tails. Perhaps you were on the mission?

David: It's a possibility. What happened next?

Heinrich: We spotted the bombers, and I was closing in on one of them when one of your Red Tails came out of the clouds and I didn't see him until it was too late. He came at me with his guns blazing, and before I could do anything about it my plane was disabled, and I was forced to eject.

David: You obviously made it out okay.

Heinrich: Yes I did. It was what happened next that I'll never forget.

David: What was that?

Heinrich: As I was floating down in my parachute two of your Red Tails approached me. A burst of machine gun fire from either one of them and it would've been all over for me. The first pilot flew by me very quickly and didn't do anything; the second pilot slowed down enough to take a closer look at me. I had the distinct feeling he was checking to see if I was okay. He gave me a quick wave, rocked the wings of his plane for me, and took off.

David: None of our pilots would shoot at a guy floating down in his parachute. We talked about that. Our mission was to destroy your aircraft, which the pilot did, and not shoot at a defenseless man.

Heinrich: All the best pilots are the same way on our side, too.

David: I did hear something about that day. I was on a different mission though.

Heinrich: Prior to the mission we were briefed by our intelligence officers about your fighter group. We knew you guys were very good and that we were in for a tough day if we were going up against the Red Tails. The reputation of your fighter group has preceded you.

David: We try to do our job.

Heinrich: Our intelligence officers told us some other interesting things about your unit.

David: Like what?

Heinrich: We know your army is segregated and that everyone in your unit from the ground crew on up to the pilots is black. And we know you've battled much discrimination at home.

David: Your briefers told you that?

Heinrich: Yes they did. It didn't surprise me. I spent some time in America and witnessed some of that discrimination myself.

David: Did they tell you anything else about my unit?

Heinrich: We know you started in North Africa, before moving to Sicily and then on to Ramitelli, Italy, where you're based now. They also told us about your commanding officer, Benjamin Davis Jr..

David: You know my commanding officer's name?

Heinrich: Yes, our intelligence officers gave us the markings of his plane and gave us specific orders to try and shoot him down if we had any opportunity to.

David: I'm shocked that your intelligence services know all this.

Heinrich: You'd be surprised what our spies know.

David: Yeah I guess I would.

Heinrich: It hasn't helped us win the war though. What made you decide to become a fighter pilot?

David: As a young kid I always loved anything to do with aviation. Whenever planes would fly overhead, I'd always look up and point at them. If I was in my house and I heard planes coming I'd run outside just to take a look at them.

Heinrich: I did much the same as a kid. Did you fly prior to the war?

David: No, there weren't a lot of opportunities for black pilots prior to the war.

Heinrich: What kind of work did you do before the war?

David: I'm a lawyer. I haven't been a lawyer for very long. After graduating from law school and passing my bar exams I worked at a law firm for just a few months before volunteering to fly planes for Uncle Sam. How about you, what did you do before the war?

Heinrich: I was a history teacher. That's how my wife and I met. She was teaching languages and I was teaching history at the same University.

David: Two educators, huh. Nothing wrong with that. My wife is also an educator.

Heinrich: What did you study as an undergraduate?

David: I majored in political science and minored in sociology.

Heinrich: I majored in history. I wanted to minor in philosophy; it was too tough of a minor, though, so I scrapped the idea.

David: Do you enjoy teaching history?

Heinrich: Yes and no.

David: Why do you say that?

Heinrich: Prior to the war the Nazis were controlling what we were allowed to teach. There were many restrictions imposed on us and it was very risky not to abide by them. I'd' enjoy teaching much more if I were allowed to teach without the restrictions.

David: Maybe it'll be that way after the war.

Heinrich: I hope so. Did you always want to be a lawyer?

David: No, I wanted to be an electrical engineer when I was younger. I was always tinkering with anything electrical I could get my hands on. I used to collect old radios that had been thrown away, take them apart, and get them working again. I made a few bucks doing that in my teens. Tinkering with electronics is still a hobby of mine; I'm glad I chose to be a lawyer though.

Heinrich: What type of law do you practice?

David: Well, as I said I wasn't a lawyer for very long before joining the armed forces. In the future I'd like to be an advocate for people who don't necessarily have access to the best legal representation. And see if maybe I can use whatever skills I have to try and make the world a better place.

Heinrich: You said you majored in political science as an undergraduate. Do you think you might end up working for your government?

David: It's a possibility. We'll have to see. I have to get back there first.

Heinrich You'll get there. So, tinkering with electronics is still a hobby of yours. Perhaps this could be a fortuitous occasion for our household.

David: Why do you say that?

Heinrich: We have two radios in this house and neither one works. They're both old, but perhaps you could get one of them to work again.

David: I'd be glad to look at them for you. Where are they?

Heinrich: They're in the living room. Maybe I should bring them in here, so you don't have to walk around too much.

David: Don't worry about it. I can get around.

Heinrich: Yes, but my wife might be upset if she comes back and sees that I've put you to work with your bad leg.

David: I'll tell her it was my idea, and that I was anxious to hear some news from the war front.

Heinrich: Okay that'll work. We'll tell her it was all your idea. She won't be mad at you. C'mon they're right in the other room.

[They move to the next room.]

SCENE 3 ▰▰▰▰▰▰▰▰▰▰▰▰▰▰▰

Heinrich: This is them.

David: They certainly are vintage models aren't they?

Heinrich: Yes they are. Will that be a problem?

David: I don't know yet. I'll need to take the back panels off both of them to see what I can do. I'll need some tools to do it.

Heinrich: I have a tool box here in the closet. I'll get it.

[Heinrich gets the tools. David takes the tools he needs to remove the back panels off both radios]

David: I think I might be able to get this one to work, but to do so, I'll need to borrow some parts from the other one. I can't make any guarantees that what I do will work.

Heinrich: If what you do doesn't work, don't worry about it, my wife and I were probably going to throw away both radios anyway.

David: All right I'll give it a try; it shouldn't take long for me to switch these parts out.

Heinrich: Do what you need to do.

[David switches the parts over.]

David: All right, that should do it. Switch on the power button now.

[The radio comes on in German.]

Heinrich: You did it.

David: I can't understand a word of what they're saying. Do you mind if I switch to the BBC?

Heinrich: Go ahead.

David: Damn! The knob to switch channels is completely stripped and I can't change stations. That's a different problem. I'll need to think about how I'm going to fix it. We'll have to stay with this station for now. What are they saying?

Heinrich: It's all propaganda. Goebbels' propaganda machine controls everything they say. According to what they're saying now everything is fine in Germany. We know that isn't true.

[Irene enters with Waldo, who attempts to climb on David.]

Irene: Careful Waldo. He's injured.

David: No worries. I love dogs. [David pets Waldo.]

Irene: I thought I heard the radio on when I was coming up the path.

Heinrich: David got it working. He happens to be an electronics expert among other things.

Irene: Why are you not in bed and resting that leg? It'll heal much faster if you keep it elevated.

David: Will do, ma'am. I really wanted to hear some news from the war front though.

Irene: Has Germany surrendered yet?

Heinrich: Not yet. Goebbels is still spewing his propaganda, and unfortunately we can't get the BBC station right now. Tuning to the BBC station is a different problem that David hasn't fixed yet.

Irene: He doesn't need to fix anything else right now.

Heinrich: C'mon David let's get back to your room.

[Both men go back to the bedroom.]

SCENE 4

David: I'd rather sit in the chair again.

Heinrich: All right, but let me get some pillows from the bed; we'll use them to elevate your leg on the ottoman.

David: If you say so.

[Irene enters. David is in a chair with his leg elevated on the ottoman.]

Irene: That's better. If you're not going to stay in bed at least keep that leg elevated for now.

Heinrich: You were gone for a long time, honey. Anything interesting happen during your walk?

Irene: No just the usual stuff. Waldo chasing birds and squirrels. It was a nice walk though.

Heinrich: Glad to hear it.

Irene: It was a long walk; I think I might take a little afternoon nap now. Do either of you need anything before I go upstairs?

David: I'm fine, thank you, ma'am.

Heinrich: We're fine. Enjoy your nap, honey.

[Irene exits.]

David: Heinrich, you two have been very nice to me, but you know as a soldier I'm obligated to try and get back to my unit as quickly as possible.

Heinrich: You're not a prisoner here—you're free to leave whenever you want. I don't think attempting to get out of Germany and back to your unit would be a very good idea now though.

David: We're not that far from Switzerland are we? Do you think there's any way I could get on a train that could get me over the border?

Heinrich: That'd be nearly impossible. There'll be Gestapo with dogs at every train station and if you somehow manage to board the train, Gestapo will be going up and down the aisles looking for suspicious passengers.

David: You're sure about that?

Heinrich: Yes, I'm very sure about that. Not only that, more
           than likely the Gestapo, or the SS, would've arrived
           to investigate your crash site a few minutes after
           we left yesterday. And it wouldn't be very difficult
           for them to figure out that the pilot had escaped
           the plane before it blew up. And the Gestapo and
           the SS are well enough informed to know that the
           Red-Tailed Mustangs are all piloted by black men,
           so they'll be on the lookout for someone fitting your
           description. That bandage on your head would be a
           dead giveaway, too.

David: You got me there.

Heinrich: You couldn't travel in your flight suit, and traveling
           in civilian clothes would be even riskier.

David: Why do you say that?

Heinrich: If you were to travel in civilian clothes and you were
           arrested by the Gestapo, your rights as a soldier
           under the Geneva Convention would be forfeited
           and you could be taken off the train and shot as
           a spy.

David: We're not all that far from Switzerland. What if I were to try and hike over those mountains to get there?

Heinrich: On that bad leg—you're not serious are you?

David: I'm hoping my leg will be better in a few days.

Heinrich: It's not a good idea. I'd offer to take you in my car, but it'd be a suicide run. There'll be several checkpoints between here and Switzerland and it would be nearly impossible to get through them. If we got caught trying to do this, we'd both probably be taken out of the car and lined up and shot.

David: I understand. I wouldn't want you to take that risk.

Heinrich: There's another reason why I don't think you should attempt to travel right now.

David: What's that?

Heinrich: Allied bombing tactics changed about two years ago. There's been increased bombing of city centers since then. This change in bombing tactics has led to a tremendous number of civilian casualties in Hamburg, Dresden, Munich, Berlin, and numerous other German cities.

David: I'm very sorry about that.

Heinrich: War is the atrocity of all atrocities isn't it? And we know who started this war—he's hiding in his bunker in Berlin. The only reason I'm telling you this is that downed pilots are in a much more dangerous situation now.

David: In what way?

Heinrich: At the beginning of the war, downed pilots captured by civilians were usually taken to the proper authorities where they were held until they could be processed and moved to POW camps. That's not always the case now though. As revenge for the bombing of our cities, angry mobs have been hunting down and killing downed pilots. I know a guy who saw it happen. A downed pilot was surrounded by an angry mob and stoned to death.

David: The fifteenth air force strictly does strategic bombing of military targets.

Heinrich: If you were surrounded by an angry mob, you wouldn't have much time to explain yourself on that. They'd identify you as an enemy pilot and you could be killed on the spot.

David: I appreciate the warning.

Heinrich: Not all German citizens are acting this way, but there's a lawlessness out there now that would make it extremely dangerous for you to travel in Germany. My wife and I discussed all this last night before we went to sleep, and we both think you should stay here for now. It's the safest place for you to be.

David: I appreciate the offer, but what if the Gestapo were to show up at your door, I could be putting you and your wife at great risk? That's not something I want to do.

Heinrich: It's very unlikely the Gestapo will show up here and it's a risk my wife and I are willing to take. You may have noticed that my wife is a humanitarian— above and beyond anything else.

David: Yeah I picked up on that yesterday.

Heinrich: This war is almost over. As a soldier you may be obligated to try and get back to your unit as quickly as you can, but you're not obligated to get yourself killed trying to do it.

David: No, I'm not.

Heinrich: You can consider this me returning the favor for when your comrades didn't fire their machine guns at me when I was floating down to the ground in my parachute.

David: Well then, I'll take you up on your offer and stay longer, but if at any point you think there's a risk to you or your wife by having me stay here, let me know and I'll head for those mountains immediately.

Heinrich: Will do. There's something else I've been curious about ever since I came up to you in your cockpit yesterday.

David: What's that?

Heinrich: When I first got to you yesterday, there were two neck chains hanging outside of your flight jacket.

David: I didn't realize that. They're both usually tucked in under my shirt.

Heinrich: That's not where they were when I got to you yesterday.

David: Hmmm. When I was in that dogfight I told you about, at one point I took my plane into a negative G as an evasive measure. Both chains must've flown out from under my shirt while I was inverted.

Heinrich: May I ask you about those chains?

David: Sure. One of them is my dog tag.

Heinrich: I kind of figured that one out. And the other one?

David: It's a chain that my grandmother gave me.

Heinrich: May I see it if you don't mind?

David: Sure.

[David pulls the chain out from under his shirt.]

Heinrich: That's a star of David isn't it?

David: Yes it is.

Heinrich: I was fairly sure that's what it was. I was somewhat
           surprised when I saw it on you yesterday.

David: Why's that?

Heinrich: I'm not sure why.

David: All four of my grandparents were Ethiopian Jews
           who immigrated to America. I was raised in the
           Jewish faith and my grandmother gave me this
           chain for my Bar Mitzvah. I've worn it at all times
           ever since then.

[There's a prolonged silence.]

Heinrich: This isn't easy for us Germans to talk about, but you know Jews are not safe in Germany now.

David: Yes, I'm aware of that. Our guys have liberated camps where awful atrocities have been committed, mostly against Jews.

Heinrich: If you were to attempt to make it to Switzerland on your own and you were arrested by the Gestapo, that chain might cause you a lot of problems.

David: It's the chance I'd have to take.

Heinrich: It's people with very sick minds that have perpetuated these crimes. We Germans should've done something to stop the rise of Hitler and the Nazis a long time ago, but we didn't.

David: I know all Germans aren't Nazis. You and your wife have been very kind to me and I'm sure there are many other Germans like you.

Heinrich: I'll let you in on a little secret.

David: Go ahead.

Heinrich: I have a great-grandmother who was Jewish.

David: Is that right? Has that ever caused you any problems?

Heinrich: I was raised as a Christian and we didn't discuss my great-grandmother outside of our family. If I'd tried to join the Nazi party they might have looked into my background, which could've caused me some problems. I never tried to join the Nazi party though. When I signed up with the Luftwaffe, they didn't ask me anything about my great grandparents and I didn't offer them any information.

David: So, you're one of us, huh. Welcome to the tribe.

Heinrich: One-eighth Jewish. That's irrelevant though. I needed all eight of those great grandparents for me to exist. Change any one of them and I wouldn't be here.

David: This is true.

Heinrich: One of my great-grandmother's daughters didn't convert from Judaism—she married a Jewish man, and they were forced to emigrate to America in the early 1930s. It's a good thing they got out when they did, or they could've been persecuted.

David: I'm glad they got out in time.

Heinrich: May I ask you a little more about some of the discrimination you've faced at home.

David: Go ahead.

Heinrich: My wife told you that her brother Joseph is being held as a prisoner of war in America.

David: Yes, she said she wants him home badly.

Heinrich: He's been allowed to send a few letters home since he's been held in America. In one of the letters he sent us, he wrote about an incident he witnessed, or that he was involved in actually. He and another German prisoner were entering a cafeteria at the same time as two black American officers. My brother-in-law and his friend were in their prisoner-of-war clothing and the two black officers were in their military uniforms. He said that he and his friend were allowed into the cafeteria, while the two black officers were denied entry. He said the black officers were very upset about it. How could they not be?

David: I'm very surprised that you're telling me this.

Heinrich: Why does it surprise you? You don't think things like that happen?

David: Oh, I know things like that happen. What surprises me is that German prisoner-of-war mail has to be censored; whoever was supposed to be censoring your brother-in-law's mail must've been sleeping on the job for that bit of information to get back to Germany.

Heinrich: Well, it did.

David: You mentioned Benjamin Davis Jr. before.

Heinrich: Yes, he's your commanding officer.

David: He went to West Point Military Academy. He was the only black cadet there. For the entire four years he was there none of his classmates would talk to him or socialize with him in any way. They called it silencing him. He never had a roommate at the academy. He ate all his meals alone. He never made one friend during the entire four years he was there. All this because of the color of his skin.

Heinrich: The human race has much work to do, doesn't it?

David: Yes it does. We have a symbol back home called the Double V, have you heard of it?

Heinrich: No, I can't say I have.

David: I suppose you wouldn't have. The Double V stands for victory against fascism abroad and victory against racism and discrimination at home.

Heinrich: You've almost achieved the first part of the Double V, good luck with the second part.

David: They may send us to fight in the Pacific after this, but thanks for the thought, we'll need it.

Heinrich: Would you like to get some rest? I can leave you alone for now.

David: That's all right, I'm not tired.

Heinrich: I'd like to get you something. I'll be back in a minute.

[Heinrich returns carrying a box.]

David: What have you got here?

Heinrich: It's a box of books. They're all written in English. Perhaps they can keep you occupied until this war ends or we can figure out how to get you out of here. Take a look and see if there's anything you might want to read.

David: Let's see, what do you have here: Rousseau, Russell, Seneca, Erasmus, Boethius, and three by Emerson.

Heinrich: Emerson is one of my all-time favorite writers. Have you read him?

David: Yes, I've read some Emerson.

Heinrich: Which of his works have you read?

David: I've read his first and second series essays and I've read some of his anti-slavery essays, too.

Heinrich: As far as I'm concerned Emerson is the greatest thing to ever come out of America.

David: Was it your stay at Harvard that got you interested in Emerson?

Heinrich: Yes it was. I took a class on transcendentalism while I was there. I really enjoyed the class and I've been hooked on Emerson ever since.

David: You know Emerson lived close to Cambridge.

Heinrich: Yes I know that. I took a day trip to see Emerson's home in Concord. It's a nice town; I also took a walk to Walden Pond to see where Emerson's friend Thoreau built his cabin while I was there.

David: I've been to Concord; it is a nice town. I'm guessing it's not just by chance that you've named your dog Waldo.

Heinrich: That is correct. I thought about naming him Emerson or Ralph, I even considered naming him Ralph Waldo Emerson.

David: That'd be a little long for a dog's name wouldn't it?

Heinrich: Yes it would. So, we settled on Waldo. It suits him best I think.

David: Yeah he's a Waldo all right. You can see that all the way.

Heinrich: Have you read any of the other authors in this box?

David: I read Rousseau's *Social Contract* and Seneca's *Letters* back during my undergraduate days. I recall both books being very good. What else do you have here…Bertrand Russell's *Conquest of Happiness*—I know the name, I haven't read anything by Russell yet though.

Heinrich: Russell's a brilliant philosopher. He's a pacifist, too. He spent six months in jail for protesting England's entry into World War 1. *Conquest of Happiness* is my favorite of his works.

David: Let's see what else you have here: *The Consolation of Philosophy* by Boethius. Wasn't Boethius thrown in prison and then he wrote about his time in prison or something like that?

Heinrich: Yes, Boethius was imprisoned on bogus charges that were politically motivated. He wrote this treatise while he was waiting to be executed. It's a brilliant work of philosophy.

David: And the last one you have here is by Erasmus.

Heinrich: Erasmus of Rotterdam has been much on my mind lately; he was a man of peace. Just about everything he wrote is infused with the need for peace.

David: *The Education of a Christian Prince* by Erasmus—it sounds more like a religious tract.

Heinrich: Erasmus was a Christian theologian; this isn't a religious tract though. There's nothing in here that would be insulting to your faith, or any other faith for that matter. *The Education of a Christian Prince* is a plea for peace more than anything else.

David: This is a nice selection of books you have here.

Heinrich: Thank you. I collect books. Most of my collection is back in Munich.

David: Every one of these authors is a philosopher, right?

Heinrich: Yes I suppose you could call them philosophers.

David: You said before that you dropped philosophy as a minor in college because you found it too difficult and yet you read all this philosophy in your spare time.

Heinrich: Perhaps I should call them wisdom writers. That might be a better way to describe these authors. I suppose it's a matter of semantics.

David: What do you mean by semantics?

Heinrich: Philosophy was originally described by the Greeks as the pursuit of wisdom; yet the wisdom writers are rarely taught in colleges now, or not by most philosophy departments, anyway.

David: What are most philosophy departments teaching now?

Heinrich: Philosophy departments are now focusing on subjects like logical positivism and logical atomism...I can barely understand a word of it.

David: Tough stuff, huh?

Heinrich: Logical positivism and logical atomism may be brilliant subjects, but they don't help me get through the day, what little I understand of them, that is. What Emerson wrote inspires me and helps me get through the day.

David: You don't have any German writers here?

Heinrich: I don't read a lot of German philosophy.

David: Why's that—do they write about logical positivism?

Heinrich: It's not that. In my first year at university, I took a class on German philosophy. The three philosophers we studied were: Nietzsche, Schopenhauer, and Kant and I found all of them difficult to read. Nietzsche is brilliant, but he philosophizes with a hammer; this is his own description of his philosophy. Schopenhauer is also brilliant—there's no denying that—and he's not that difficult to understand either, but he's such a pessimist I can only read him in small doses. Kant might be one of the brightest minds that's ever existed, but he's extremely difficult to understand.

David: O for three, huh. Was that what made you decide not to minor in philosophy?

Heinrich: It had something to do with it. Emerson is easier going than our German philosophers. Perhaps it's a reflection of your country.

David: You don't have any fiction here either. Do you like fiction?

Heinrich: Yes, I like fiction very much. Fiction can be a great escape at times. Fiction reaches a much wider audience, too. Erich Marie Remarque's *All Quiet on the Western Front* might be the most widely read anti-war book ever written. It was so popular here in Germany, the Nazis had it banned.

David: Yeah I read about the Nazis burning books.

Heinrich: Other books were banned. *All Quiet on the Western Front* was on the top of the list of books the Nazis banned though. They said it was unpatriotic and portrayed the German Army in a poor light, when all it really did was describe the horrors of war. Kipling once wrote that if history were taught in the form of stories, it would never be forgotten. I think there's much truth to that.

David: You're obviously opposed to war; how is it that you ended up becoming a fighter pilot?

Heinrich: Yes, I am opposed to war. Military service is compulsory here in Germany. If I hadn't volunteered to join the Luftwaffe, at some point I would've received a knock on my door and been dragged down to the recruiter's office where I probably would've been given a beating and then sent off as an infantryman to Stalingrad or some other place like that. I wanted to avoid that from happening, and like yourself I love to fly, so I joined the Luftwaffe.

David: I can't say I blame you for that.

Heinrich: Do you think mankind will ever stop going to war?

David: Tough question. I would hope so.

Heinrich: In the last 3,000 years of recorded history there have been very few times where there wasn't a war going on somewhere in the world.

David: As a history teacher you would know better than I would about that.

Heinrich: I'm not trying to lessen Germany's responsibility for this war. We let a madman take charge of our country and look at what it's led to. What I want to know is how can something like this be prevented from ever happening again?

David: You would hope the human race has learned its lesson after this one.

Heinrich: Millions of lives lost, millions more with their lives forever shattered. Soldiers with amputated limbs, children with amputated limbs. And mankind keeps doing this to itself over and over again. What can be done to prevent something like this from ever happening again.

David: People have to choose better leaders, leaders who won't take their countries to war. The whole world needs to do the same. I know that probably sounds like a simplified answer and easier said than done.

Heinrich: Sometimes I want to break it down to the lowest common denominator and go from there.

David: What do you mean by the lowest common denominator?

Heinrich: How do you create better people? I mean more good people in the world and less bad people.

David: That's a really tough question.

Heinrich: We let an evil megalomaniac take charge of our country. That evil megalomaniac couldn't have done what he did alone—he needed an inner circle of very evil people like Hess, Himmler, Goebbels and Goering. Where does evil like that come from?

David: I'm surprised you're asking me that. We Americans have been wondering about that for a long time.

Heinrich: I know it seems like an impossible question to answer, but can you give me any help on this? We Germans obviously haven't figured it out yet.

David: To me everything starts with the family. I think hate is learned at home and hate in the extreme can lead to evil.

Heinrich: So, you think it all starts with the family?

David: Yes I do.

Heinrich: Please tell me more of your thoughts on this?

David: You know what has always upset me the most? Bullies. Seeing bullies pick on weaker people makes my blood boil, it always has.

Heinrich: I don't like bullies either.

David: If you ask people just about everyone will tell you they hate bullies. Yet every generation keeps producing new ones. That kind of behavior is learned at home. There can be terrible repercussions for children who are emotionally or physically abused by their parents. I don't know anything about the backgrounds of Hitler or any of his inner circle, but I can just about guarantee you they all had some kind of an authoritarian upbringing, with one kind of abuse or another attached to it. And more than likely they were taught hate at home, too.

Heinrich: You really think so huh?

David: Yes I do, and my experience with haters is that sooner or later they'll tell you they hate everybody. You just have to wait your turn.

Heinrich: That's most definitely true with Hitler. In the beginning Hitler said he hated the Bolsheviks, Jews, Poles, Gypsies, and Slavs. Now he hates his own generals because they couldn't go out and conquer the world for him. Word has it that he hates the German people now, too—they're not good enough for him. Hess was his right-hand man and Hitler has said that he'd put Hess in front of a firing squad if he ever set foot on German soil again. And word has it that he recently had Goering put under house arrest, too.

David: Like I said, with haters you just have to wait your turn.

Heinrich: Suppose these theories of yours are true, what could ever be done about the situation?

David: Tough question. Telling people how to raise their children isn't an easy thing to do.

Heinrich: True.

David: I don't have any children and I'm sure it's not easy raising them. I know there's no one way to do it. Some parents are going to be stricter than others, and within reason, that's perfectly fine. Parents need to discipline their children sometimes. My parents pushed me hard to do well in school, and if they didn't think I was trying hard enough, they let me know about it. Now, I'm glad they did that. One set of parents might raise their kids on hunting and fishing, while the next set of parents might raise their kids on piano recitals and visiting museums and that's perfectly fine, too. There just has to be one constant throughout it all.

Heinrich: And with that one constant you think you can rid the world of evil.

David: I don't know if it'll solve all the world's problems, it wouldn't hurt to try though.

Heinrich: No, it wouldn't.

David: What's a bad regime, it's just a bunch of bullies multiplied by a hundred or a thousand, isn't it?

Heinrich: I never looked at it that way.

David: You're the first German I've talked to since I've gotten to Europe. If you don't mind my asking— how do you explain Hitler and the Nazi rise to power in Germany?

Heinrich: No, I don't mind you asking. I can tell you some of the political side of it. The Treaty of Versailles wasn't a very good deal for Germany. That was followed by rampant inflation and very high unemployment. Germans were desperate for solutions when Hitler and the Nazis came along with their propaganda machine promising solutions to these problems. When the economy started to improve, Hitler and the Nazis got credit for it.

David: A lot of that improvement to the economy came from building up the armament industries, didn't it?

Heinrich: Yes it did and look where that got us.

David: I don't take lightly the need for good government. People have to be careful who they choose to be their leaders. Good governments can lift a lot of people up and bad governments can bring a lot of people down.

Heinrich: That's for sure.

[Irene enters.]

Irene: It sounds as if the two of you are having an interesting conversation.

Heinrich: You're awake. Yes, we've been discussing how to put an end to war.

Irene: What the world needs is to put more women in power. Men have made a mess of things for far too long. No offense against men, David.

David: No offense taken ma'am. And it's not a bad idea either.

Irene: I see you've brought David several books.

Heinrich: Yes we've been discussing books, too.

Irene: Let me see what books you've brought him. [She looks at the collection.] These are very good books, but if you really want to enlighten David, you should have him read authors like Jane Addams or Zora Neale Hurston.

Heinrich: We don't have anything by Jane Addams or Zora Neale Hurston in the house, and recommending authors that I've never read myself would be a bit insincere don't you think?

Irene: Well, you ought to start reading more female authors then, it would do you a lot of good.

Heinrich: Duly noted.

Irene: Are you two hungry?

Heinrich: Yes I'm hungry.

Irene: And you, David?

David: Whenever you two want to eat is fine with me.

Irene: If it's okay with you two, I'm just going to heat up some leftovers from yesterday.

David: That's fine with me. What we had yesterday was delicious.

Irene: All right, it shouldn't take long then.

[Irene exits.]

Heinrich: My wife and I have an ongoing debate about all things literary, like who's better: Jane Austen or

Charles Dickens. She's with Austen and I'm with Dickens.

David: Diversity is a good thing. Have you ever read anything by W.E.B. Dubois or Frederick Douglass?

Heinrich: No, I can't say I have.

David: Dubois was the first black American to earn a PhD from your alma mater, Harvard. He's never written a bad sentence. He and Douglass are my two favorites.

Heinrich: I'll make it a point to read both of them the first chance I get.

David: You should do that.

[Irene steps back into the room.]

Irene: If David's going to stay where he is to eat, we'll need a third chair in here.

David: I'll drop my leg down so we can use the ottoman as a table again.

Irene: Fine. Heinrich, after you get the other chair could you move the pillows back to the bed and cover the ottoman with linen again.

Heinrich: Will do honey.

Irene: Good. I'll be back in a few minutes with the food.

[Irene enters with a plate of food for David.]

Irene: Heinrich, can you help me bring the rest in.

Heinrich: Yes, dear.

[Irene and Heinrich bring in the rest of the food along with a pitcher of water. They all start eating.]

Irene: We told you about our family yesterday David, why don't you tell us about yours now?

David: Well as I said yesterday, I'm married and we don't have any children yet.

Irene: Tell us about growing up in Boston then?

David: I had one sister whom I'm very close with and my parents are great.

Irene: I'd like to hear more if you don't mind?

David: What can I say, Mom was an angel—she pretty much ran the show around the house; Dad was my role model, and he was a real good one at that.

Irene: Keep going please.

Heinrich: When my dad saw how much I enjoyed seeing planes fly overhead he started taking me to the airport on his day off. We had to take a ferry ride to get there, and we'd stay there all day just watching planes take off and land. My sister and mother weren't interested in going with us for that. I couldn't get enough of it though. Dad would buy me a burger and soda pop while we were there. They're great memories.

Irene: That sounds very nice. Please tell us more.

David: You sure you want to hear more of this?

Irene: Yes we do.

David: My parents got me a model airplane for Christmas one year when I was a kid. I think I was about seven at the time. That memory stands out. I grew up during the Depression and we didn't get a lot of toys for Christmas. There were always a few gifts under the tree for us—they were mostly necessities like clothes though.

Irene: It was hard here in Germany, too.

David: It was Mom who picked out the model airplane and Dad helped me build it. I'll always remember that gift. As I've gotten older, I realize how hard my parents worked just to put a few gifts under the tree. And even more important than what was under the tree is what filled the room, every crevice of the room.

Irene: I had a feeling you were raised like that. You should start your own family as soon as you get back to America.

David: My wife and I are planning to do that.

Irene: Do you think you'll raise your family in Boston?

David: I'm not sure. My wife has relatives in Washington, D.C., and a lot of the work I'd like to do is based in D.C., so we could end up there.

Irene: I'm sure you'll do fine wherever you end up. I don't mean to be rude gentlemen, but my spring allergies have kicked in and I think I'm going to call it an early night.

Heinrich: You shouldn't have taken such a long walk in the woods today. You know what April does to you.

Irene: I'll be fine. I just need a little extra rest tonight. C'mon Heinrich, let's bring these plates to the kitchen and you and David can have some strudel.

Heinrich: You won't be joining us for strudel?

Irene: I'll pass tonight. You two can enjoy your strudel and continue your conversation.

[After clearing the plates, Irene returns with two dessert plates of strudel and Heinrich follows her in with two cups of tea.]

Irene: All right you two, enjoy your dessert, I'm going upstairs now. Good night, David.

Heinrich: Good night, ma'am.

Irene: Heinrich, please take the dessert plates to the kitchen and rinse them before you come upstairs.

Heinrich: Will do.

David: This strudel is very good.

Heinrich: Yes it is, isn't it.

David: You should go up and join your wife after we finish this dessert.

Heinrich: I don't mind keeping you company for a little longer.

David: Actually, I was looking forward to doing a little reading after you leave.

Heinrich: Oh yeah, which of these books do you think you'll read?

David: They're your books—why don't you make a recommendation for me.

Heinrich: You said you've read Emerson, Rousseau, and Seneca before, so why not give one of the authors you haven't read yet a try?

David: That sounds like a good idea. That would leave Russell, Boethius, and Erasmus to choose from. C'mon it's your collection, I'll go with what you recommend.

Heinrich: All three of these books are very good, but it's Erasmus who's been on my mind the most lately.

David: You said he was a man of peace.

Heinrich: Yes he was, but he was so much more than that.

David: In what way?

Heinrich: Erasmus was the most learned man in all of Europe during his time, so much so that during the last decade of his life, they calculated that somewhere between 10 and 20 percent of all the books published in Europe were either written by Erasmus or were works that had plagiarized his.

David: Europe is a big continent, that's saying a lot.

Heinrich: Yes it is. And just about everything he wrote was infused with the need to avoid war at all costs. He also wrote a treatise called *Complaint of Peace* that's brilliant. It's a dialogue where the protagonist is Peace itself and Peace complains throughout the dialogue that no one ever listens to him and that people all too often choose war over peace.

David: Prescient to say the least, huh.

Heinrich: Yes it is. I don't have my copy of *Complaint of Peace* here; it's in Munich. As good as *Complaint of Peace* is, his *Education of a Christian Prince* is my favorite of all his works.

David: Erasmus sounds like an author that the Nazis would've banned.

Heinrich: Erasmus' writings weren't on the Nazis' radar or not very high on their list anyway.

David: Why's that?

Heinrich: Because Erasmus isn't read very often these days, the Nazis wouldn't have been paying much attention to his works like the way they did with Remarque's *All Quiet on the Western Front*.

David: Got it.

Heinrich: *Education of a Christian Prince* is just a little over a hundred pages long…a lawyer like yourself might be able to finish it in one pop.

David: I don't know about that. I'll give it a shot though.

Heinrich: All right then, I'll leave you alone so you can get started on it. Let me clear these plates. Do you need anything else before I go upstairs?

David: No, I'm good, thanks.

Heinrich: Well then, good night, David. See you in the morning.

David: Good night, Heinrich.

ACT TWO

SCENE 1 ▬▬▬▬▬▬▬▬▬▬▬▬

[It's the following morning and the radio is playing in the living room. Heinrich knocks on David's bedroom door.]

Heinrich: Are you awake? There's been some big news announced on the radio.

David: Yes, I'm awake, I'll come out to the living room.

Heinrich: You ready for this. Hitler committed suicide last night.

David: He did?

Heinrich: Yeah, he did.

David: Does this mean the war's over?

Heinrich: I'm not sure yet. Hitler appointed Karl Donitz to be his successor. He's the head of the Navy. According to what they're saying on the radio, Donitz has sent emissaries to Eisenhower's headquarters to negotiate a peace settlement. Goebbel might be dead, too. The news on the radio seemed more accurate this morning. It's great news, right?

David: Yes it is. There's something I wanted to talk to you about though.

Heinrich: What's that?

David: Did you hear that artillery last night; it's moved a lot closer in the last 24 hours.

Heinrich: How could we not have heard it?

David: That has to be Allied artillery and it can't be coming from more than 20 miles from here.

Heinrich: It's most definitely Allied artillery. The Allies are crossing Germany at a very rapid pace now. I wouldn't know if it's American or British artillery, but that wouldn't make much of a difference to you would it?

David: No, it wouldn't. If they're only 20 miles away I might be able to walk to the Allied lines by now.

Heinrich: Walking 20 miles with your bad leg would be a little difficult for you right now, don't you think. I could probably get you there by car, but there's just one problem preventing me from doing that.

David: What's that? Do you think the Gestapo or the SS would stop us on the way?

Heinrich: It's not that. I think the Gestapo and the SS will be heading away from the Allied artillery and they won't be anywhere near here now. The problem is that my wife and I don't want to see you leave.

David: I appreciate you wanting me to stay, but I'd really like to get to the Allied lines.

Heinrich: I knew you would.

David: It's not that I don't appreciate your hospitality. It's just that there are numerous reasons why I'd like to get back to Allied lines. For one, I'm not sure how long they wait before they contact my wife to let her know I went missing in action. If they've let her know already, I'd like to get word to her as soon as possible that I'm okay. The guys in my unit will be worried about me, too—they don't know if I made it out alive. I'd like to get word to them that I'm okay.

Heinrich: We understand all that. My wife anticipated that you'd want to get going as soon as possible. She had some old flour bags stored in a closet and she cut them up to make white flags out of them earlier this morning. She's outside tying them to the car right now.

David: Why don't we go out and help her.

Heinrich: She wanted to do it herself. She says if you need a job done right you should have a woman do it.

David: I won't argue with her on that.

Heinrich: She told me she would come in and get us when she was finished. Before you leave we have a few gifts for you. My wife put together a package of food for you—she has that outside for you—and I found a few more books around the house that are written in English. I'd like you to have them.

David: You don't have to do that. I know how much you love books; you should keep them for your collection.

Heinrich: It's too late, I've already inscribed both books to you. Here, take them.

David: All right, if you insist…let's see what you have here? Rousseau's *Emile*.

Heinrich: You said you read Rousseau's *Social Contract* and you liked it. Have you read *Emile*?

David: No, I haven't.

Heinrich: Rousseau was one of the world's great geniuses. *Emile* is one of his most artistic works, and it's less political than his *Social Contract*.

David: Well, thank you.

Heinrich: I have a good Kant story for you, it's about Rousseau's *Emile*.

David: Let's hear it.

Heinrich: So, Kant lived his entire adult life in Konigsberg. And every day at exactly 3:30 he'd take a walk. Whether it was raining or snowing, it didn't matter; at exactly 3:30, he would leave his house and set out for his walk. The people of Konigsberg grew so accustomed to seeing Kant take his daily walk at 3:30 they said they could set their watches by it. And then after he did this every single day, year after year, the people of Konigsberg didn't see Kant for several days and they started to worry about him. "There must be something wrong with Kant they said, we haven't seen him in days. Is Kant ill?" Kant wasn't ill though.

David: No

Heinrich: No, he wasn't ill. Kant had received a copy of Rousseau's *Emile* and he took the time to read it through twice after receiving it. And that was why the people of Konigsberg didn't see him for several days.

David: It's a fairly thick book, Kant read it twice through, huh?

Heinrich: Kant said he read it through once to appreciate the book's message and a second time to appreciate the book's artistry. I can't understand much of Kant's writing—his genius is up in the stratosphere—but I can understand his appreciation of Rousseau's *Emile*. Kant and I are in agreement on *Emile*. You've got another book there.

David: Montaigne's essays.

Heinrich: Montaigne pretty much invented the essay—to this day he's still arguably the greatest essayist that's ever written.

David: When did he write these essays?

Heinrich: In the late 1600s. He lived in France. He wrote over 100 essays…they're all good. This is a select copy of 29 of his best essays.

David: I know how much books mean to you, so I'll cherish these gifts.

Heinrich: I put a slip of paper inside Montaigne's essays that has our address here and our address in Munich on it.

David: Let me get my stuff and I'll write my home address down for you.

[David returns with his flight bag and a slip of paper in his hand.]

David: Here's my parents' address. I might relocate depending upon where I end up getting a job. My parents aren't going anywhere though.

[Irene enters the door with Waldo.]

Irene: The car is ready. Are you ready to go, David?

David: Yes, I'm ready.

Irene: Have you exchanged addresses?

Heinrich: It's done.

Irene: There's a package on the front seat with some food
            in it. There's some strudel in there and a few other
            things. I've tied a white flag to the hood ornament
            of the car and another white flag to the front grill,
            and here's a third white flag that you can wave out
            the window as you approach the Allied lines.

Heinrich: They're not going to be worried about a car like ours.
            If it looks dangerous I'll let David out a quarter mile
            away from the Allied lines and he can walk the rest
            of the way there by himself.

Irene: With that bad leg of his you should try to get him
            as close to the Allied lines as possible.

David: I'll be hanging out the window and waving this
            white flag as we pull up. They won't bother us.

Irene: Will we see you again?

David: I'll make it a point to get over here and to see you
            again. And you can visit me in America any time
            you want. Bring your kids with you.

Irene: We'll miss you. Waldo's going to miss you, too.

David: I'm not going to forget what the two of you have
            done for me.

Heinrich: We should get going.

[Irene and David hug, David and Heinrich walk to the car.
Irene waves as they leave.]

The End

...